CooolZ

MW00873849

GOODNIGHT, MY GOLF

BEDTIME GOLF STORY
FOR BOYS

Goodnight, my Golf. Bedtime golf story for boys. Cooolz Ltd., 2021. 32 p., illustrated.

ISBN 978-9934-9022-3-9

Publisher Cooolz Ltd.
Author Janina Spruza

Copyright © Cooolz Ltd.
Copyright © Use of characters, images, this book's idea or text without the author's permission is prohibited.

Once upon a time, there lived a little boy.

The window of his bedroom overlooked a golf course.

Every evening before going to bed, he looked out of the window, thinking:

Why are there so many people?

What are they doing?

What is going on there?

One night, while the boy was playing with his toys, a real star flew into his window.

On the star there sat an amazing guest.

He was round and yellow and very merry looking.

Hi, little one!
My name is Par.

Every night I see you watching the golf course.
And today I want to invite you to a real magic golf world.
But first, please accept my present.

These are golf clubs. With them, you will discover
the miracles that live in our fairy tale.

With a little giggle, Par snapped his fingers, and suddenly a magic car appeared in the middle of the room.

It had wheels, wings, and even an illuminated air cushion.

They hopped in the magic car and in an instant, they found themselves on the golf course.

Well-dressed people were walking around, hitting a little ball with their golf clubs.

This is a golf course,
and the people you see are golfers. We call them golf players.
They all have the same goal.

They try to hit the ball into a hole from the starting point,
or tee, in as few strokes as possible.

Par gave the boy a ball and a club, and they stopped by the tee of the first hole.

By the way, I forgot to introduce myself properly.

Though you know my name, you don't know who I am.

I am Par, and par stands for a golf game score.

In our game, the score depends on the number of strokes that a player takes to hit the ball into the hole from the tee.

The boy made several strokes and finally hit his ball into the hole.
Suddenly, a beautiful girl with little magic birds flitting around her appeared by the golf hole.

Hi! My name is Birdie.

Just like Par, I am a good golf game score.

You can call me the princess of golf.

You played well, so I want to give you a present.

Birdie handed the boy one of her little birds and it fluttered up to sit on his shoulder.

This bird will cheer you up if you ever feel sad during the game. Hurry up, there are many other miracles waiting for you. If you are lucky, you may see the king of golf himself.

Par and the boy got back in their car and drove it to the next hole.

The boy played well again, and at the moment his ball rolled into the cup, a character that looked like an eagle appeared.

Hi! My name is Eagle.

Just like Par and Birdie, I am a very good golf game score.

You are doing great! Well done!

Please, take this magic golden golf ball and keep it as a lucky charm.

The boy played several more holes, but no miracles happened.

He felt sad and started crying. Birdie's bird started to sing a merry song.

At the next hole, the boy sank the ball into the cup in a couple of strokes, and then, as if by magic, a wonderfully elegant character appeared.

I am Albatross. Like my friends Par, Birdie, and Eagle, I am a very very good golf game score. Getting me is real magic!

I see that you are excellent at golf.

Take my gift: This is a magic umbrella.

It will protect you from rain and bright sun on the golf course.

Hurry up to see the other miracles.

If you do, you may be lucky enough to see the king of golf himself.

At last, they stood by the tee of the 18th hole, which is the final hole. The boy swung the club and hit the ball right into the cup with a single stroke.

Fireworks started going off all at once, and everything around them began to sparkle and shine with lights, as if in a real fairy tale.

From these lights, the one and only king of golf, the very best golf score, appeared.

He looked gorgeous, and on his head, he wore a crown shaped like a golf cap. The boy had never seen such a crown before.

I am Hole-in-One, the King of Golf.

Only the best and the luckiest players can see me!

And you were lucky today, which means that miracles can always happen.

I want to give you a royal gift— my magic cap crown.

It doesn't only bring you luck, it will also help you find the royal wisdom of golf and become the best player in the world!

Then Birdie, Eagle, and Albatross appeared.

Together with Hole-in-One and Par, they lifted the boy up and started tossing him in the air as if he was a real hero.

Now it's time to go home. We will be waiting for you here on the golf course.

Bring your parents and grandparents. Here on the golf course you will find lots of new friends.

But now it's time to sleep. Your little bed has been waiting for you.

Par snapped his fingers, and the little boy found himself back in his room.

There was a knock-knock on the door, and his mom and dad looked in.

Daddy, Mommy!
This was the best adventure ever!
I saw so many miracles today!

Just look how many magic presents I've got!

Please promise me that you will take me to play golf tomorrow!

This is the best place in the world!

And the best game ever!

Let's play golf with all our family, and you will see this fairy tale too!

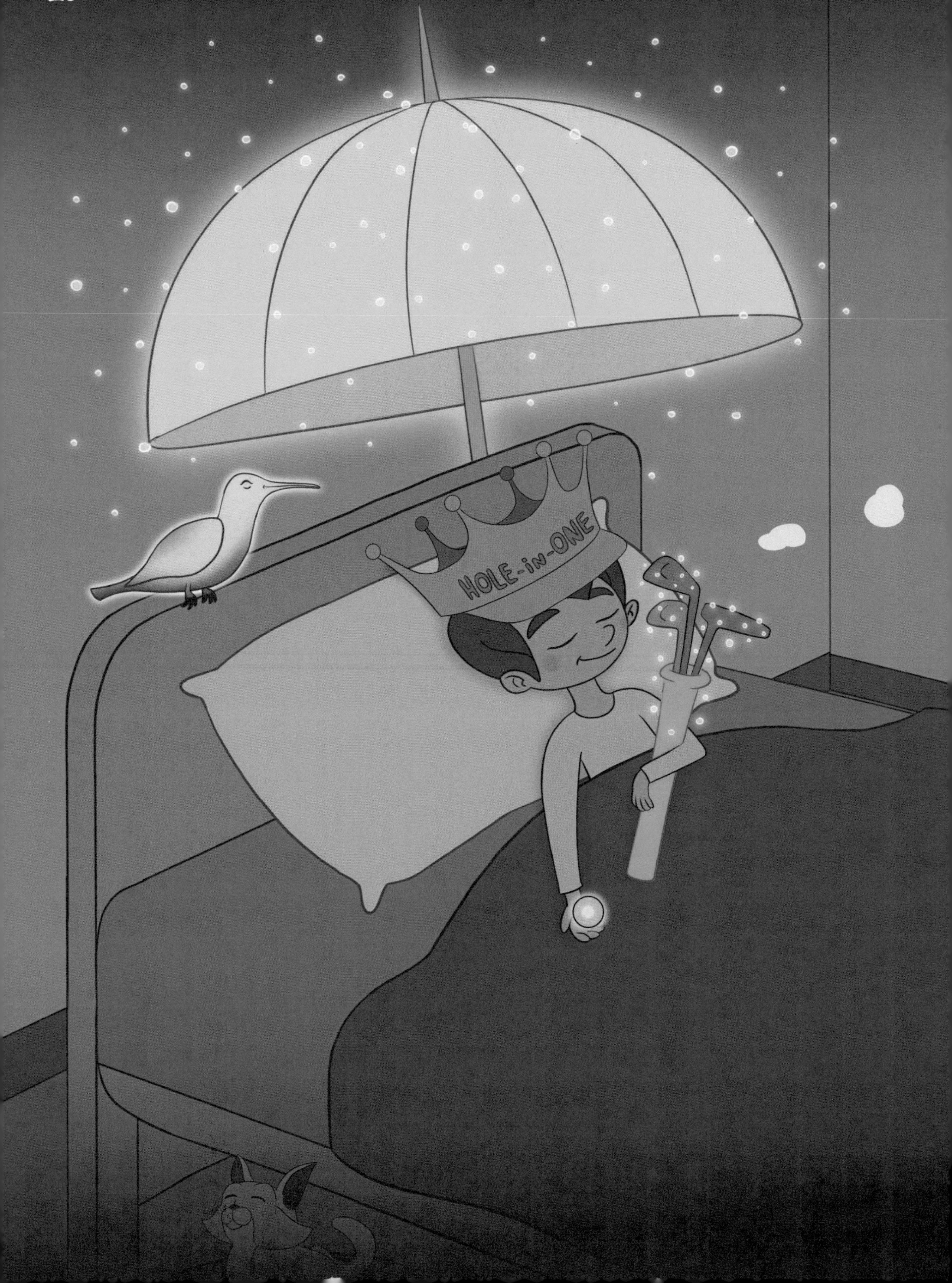
HOLE-in-ONE

Good night, my dear friends Par, Birdie, Eagle, Albatross, and Hole-in-One!

Good night, my magic golf course!

Good night, my golf!

The boy put Hole-in-One's cap on his head, fixed the magic umbrella over his bed, tucked himself under the blanket, took the magic ball in one hand, hugged his golf club bag, and fell asleep, smiling.

Birdie's little bird slept on the headboard.

All night he dreamed of playing golf with his new friends, Par, Birdie, Eagle, Albatross, and Hole-in-One.

Color it!

Meet all the books published by CooolZ

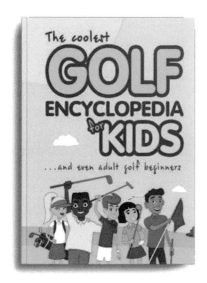

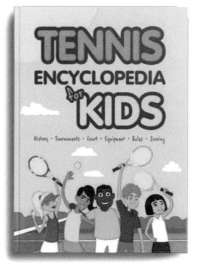

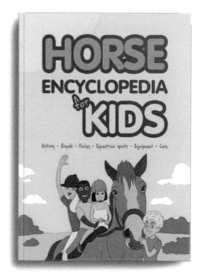

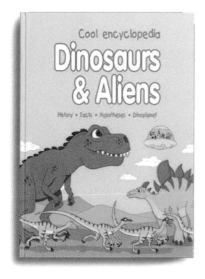

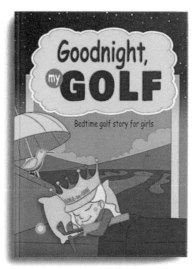

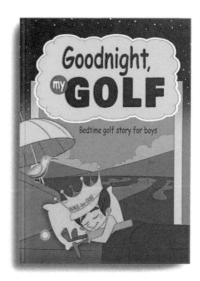

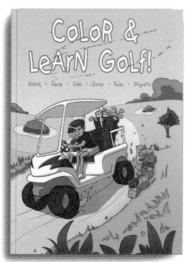

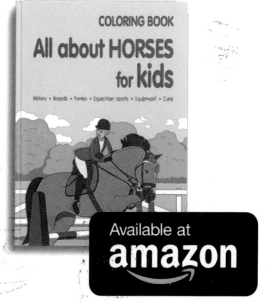

Available at amazon

Goodnight, my Golf. Bedtime golf story for boys

Cooolz Ltd., 2021. 32 p., illustrated.

Author Janina Spruza

ISBN 978-9934-9022-3-9

Copyright © Cooolz Ltd.
Copyright © Use of characters, images, this book's idea or text
without the author's permission is prohibited.

Made in the USA
Middletown, DE
16 April 2022

64334414R00020